MATHNET™ CASEBOOK

#6 The Case of the Smart Dummy

By David D. Connell and Jim Thurman

Illustrated by Danny O'Leary

Scientific American

BOOKS FOR YOUNG READERS

Children's Television Workshop

W. H. Freeman/New York

Scientific American Books for Young Readers
is an imprint of W.H. Freeman and Company,
41 Madison Avenue, New York, New York 10010

On **MATHNET**, the role of George Frankly is played by
Joe Howard; the role of Pat Tuesday is played by Toni Di Buono;
the role of Benny Pill is played by Barry K. Willerford; the role
of Sergeant Abruzzi is played by Michael Sergio; the role of
Captain Joe Grecco is played by Emilio Del Pozo; the roles of
Edgar Bergman and Charlie McShtick are played by Todd Stockman.

Cover photo of Joe Howard, Toni Di Buono, and Todd Stockman
© CTW/Richard Termine

Illustrated by Danny O'Leary
Activities illustrated by Sarah Albee

Library of Congress Cataloging-in-Publication Data

Connell, David D.

The case of the smart dummy: a Mathnet Casebook / by David
D. Connell and Jim Thurman.

p. cm.

Summary: Using clues derived from mathematical knowledge,
Mathnet detectives Pat Tuesday and George Frankly solve a case
involving a ventriloquist's stolen dummy and a suitcase filled
with counterfeit money.

ISBN 0-7167-6556-X (hard)—ISBN 0-7167-6557-8 (soft)

[1. Mystery and detective stories. 2. Ventriloquism—Fiction.]

PZ7.C761853Cap 1995

[Fic]—dc20   94-1865

                                                          CIP

                                                          AC

Printed in the United States of America

10 9 8 7 6 5 4 3 2 1

CHAPTER
1

Pat Tuesday was glad to get out of the morning rain, but she struggled collapsing her umbrella at NYPD Headquarters. In the process, she managed to spray water all over Sergeant Abruzzi, who seemed pleased at the attention.

Pat headed for the Mathnet offices, but she paused when she heard voices behind the door. One belonged to George Frankly, Pat's partner. The other was an odd, squeaky voice that Pat did not recognize.

"I've been around a lot of sadness lately," Pat heard the squeaky voice say.

"You have?"

"Oh, yes. I had my flu shot yesterday."

"Really?" George asked.

"Yeah. I had to. It broke its leg."

Pat heard George giggle. She was puzzled. Usually it was George telling the bad jokes at Mathnet.

"But the news hasn't been all that bad," the odd voice continued. "I just signed a contract with MGM."

"That's terrific."

"Yeah. Now all I gotta do is get *them* to sign it."

Pat had had enough. She threw open the door and saw George sitting on the edge of a desk, snickering.

Slumped in the chair next to George sat a man wearing rumpled clothing and a blank stare. It wasn't the sight of the man gazing vacantly into space that caused Pat to stop in her tracks—it was the ventriloquist's dummy laughing hysterically along with George.

"Oh, Pat. Come in," George greeted his partner. "Charlie here was just doing some material from his comedy routine." George waved a hand at the dummy.

Pat's mouth was agape. "Charlie . . . ?"

"Charlie McShtick." George made the introductions. "Charlie, meet my partner, Pat Tuesday."

"It's a pleasure, Ms. Tuesday," Charlie's squeaky voice answered. "And meet my ventriloquist, Edgar Bergman." Charlie nodded toward the vacant-eyed man in the chair.

"Nice to meet you, Charlie. And you, Edgar . . ." Pat waved her hand in front of Edgar's face. Nothing.

"Edgar's a dummy, Pat. I mean he isn't talking . . . at the moment," George spluttered. "He *was*, but . . ."

"That's why we're here," Charlie interrupted.

"Where are you usually?" Pat asked. A minute later she was sorry she asked.

"Well, I was born in California," Charlie began.

"Where?" George picked up his cue.

"Sequoia National Park."

"When?"

"Ash Wednesday."

"Ever pine for it?"

"Occasionally I balsam."

Pat took a deep breath and raised her voice: "All right, you two. Enough! What the heck is going on here?" George and Charlie jumped, but Edgar remained unmoved.

"Charlie and Edgar were here when I got here, Pat," George said.

Waving her hand in front of Edgar again, Pat said, "I don't think Edgar *is* here."

"That's the point," George said. "Charlie, tell her."

"The dummy is going to tell me what's wrong, and Edgar is going to sit there?" Pat asked in disbelief.

"That's right."

Pat rolled her eyes but picked up her notebook. "Does Edgar drink a glass of water while Charlie talks?"

Charlie took a deep breath. Edgar didn't. "Ms. Tuesday, I know this seems strange, but we used to be 'Charlie, Edgar and Lolly,' a terrific act."

"Used to be?" Pat asked, scribbling in her notebook.

"Yes, ma'am. Until Lolly turned up missing. That's why we're not doing the ASFAS Benefit." Charlie paused.

"ASFAS?"

"The Award Show for the Award Shows," Charlie explained.

"Is that the show that gives awards to the shows that give awards to the shows that get awards?"

"That's right, Pat," George nodded. "ASFAS rewards shows like the Oscars, the Emmys, the Tonys, the Patsys, the Aces, the Grammys, the Yorkies . . ."

"The Yorkies?" Pat asked.

"The award for the most unusual pizza topping." Charlie grinned, showing off pearly, but wooden, teeth.

George continued the story.

"Anyway, Pat, Edgar and his act were going to host the show."

"But Lolly is missing?" Pat said.

Charlie's wooden smile vanished. "We had just come back from a bunch of one-nighters in the Midwest. . . ."

"One nighters?" Pat looked at George for help.

"In show biz, a one-nighter means you play each night in a different city," George explained.

"Anyway, when we got off the plane in New York, Lolly was missing," Charlie said. "Without Lolly, the act is ruined. ASFAS must have heard, because they canceled us."

As Charlie spoke, Pat watched Edgar. The ventriloquist was still motionless and vacant, a complete contrast to his enthusiastic dummy. It was a little spooky.

"So where is Lolly?" Pat asked. "She couldn't have gotten off the plane in midair, could she?"

"No, ma'am," Charlie said. "The way we travel is, Edgar flies first class and Lolly and I don't."

"Do you fly coach?" George asked.

"Nope."

"Economy?" Pat tried.

"Baggage," Charlie said, glancing at George.

"Sounds uncomfortable," said George, sensing a gag.

"It's okay. I sleep like a log." Charlie and George snickered until Pat called them to order. Charlie went on.

"Lolly and I go in two suitcases, and Edgar picks us up off the baggage carousel. It's uncomfortable, but we get Frequent Suitcase Miles and sometimes we upgrade to under the seat." Charlie stopped and blinked a few times, his eyelids making tiny clicking sounds. "This time, when we got to LaGuardia Airport, I was there, but Lolly wasn't."

Pat reached out to give Charlie a pat on the shoulder. Then she remembered he was a dummy. She pulled back and began writing busily. "Was the bag gone?"

"No," Charlie answered. "Edgar picked up both cases. We got to the apartment, he opened my suitcase up, then he opened Lolly's and . . ."

Charlie began to get even more emotional. Edgar didn't even blink.

". . . and Edgar just said, 'Oh, no! It's the wrong bag.' Then he slammed it shut and hasn't spoken since." Charlie gave a shaky sigh.

Pat stared at Charlie, then Edgar. She shook her head. "This is bizarre!"

"Yes it is, Pat, but go along with it," George whispered. "Charlie needs our help."

"I think Edgar needs it more," Pat mumbled. She turned back to the dummy. "Charlie, what was in the other bag?"

"Beats me." Charlie seemed to shrug. "Edgar closed it. I heard a couple of clicks and that's all she wrote."

"Where's the bag?" George asked.

"In our apartment, Mr. Frankly."

There was a pause as Pat, George and Charlie looked at one another, then at the lifeless-looking Edgar.

"Shall we?" George asked.

"Okay," Pat said, "but only if *you* sign the report."

* * *

With Edgar trailing, Charlie escorted George and Pat to a brownstone apartment house called The Broken Arms. Edgar's home was filled with autographed photos of celebrities the act had worked with over the years.

"Boy, Charlie. You know a lot of famous people," George said in awe.

"Yep. Unfortunately, that kind of thing happens

when you've been in the business as long as we have."

Without thinking, George turned to Edgar. "Where's the bag?"

But Edgar just stared at the wall.

Charlie answered instead, nodding toward a table nearby. Pat and George stepped up for a closer look.

"It's got a combination lock," Pat remarked.

"Three cylinders, each with digits zero through nine," George noted. "That's a lot of possibilities."

"Ten digits, three cyclinders." Pat calculated. "Ten to the third power. One *thousand* possibilities."

"What are you guys talking about?" asked Charlie.

"The different number of settings this lock has," Pat said. "We might have to try one thousand combinations to find the right one. It could take a while."

"Wait a minute, Pat," George said, remembering something. "If this isn't Edgar's bag, how the heck did he get it open before?"

They looked at Edgar, who was still staring at the wall. He sure wasn't talking. That left the dummy.

"Maybe the case wasn't locked before," Pat noted. "Charlie, didn't you say that when Edgar closed the bag, you heard *two* clicks?"

"I'd swear on my mother's bark."

George held up one finger. "Then one click happened when Edgar closed the latch."

"Right," Pat nodded, "and the other might have been when he moved a cylinder, and locked the case."

"If that happened he may have changed only one digit," George said excitedly. "The case would still be locked, but we'd have only *six* possibilities."

"Why six?" Charlie asked.

Pat pointed to the lock. It was set on 6 3 8. "One click means Edgar changed only one of these three digits, moving it either one digit up or down."

"I get it!" Charlie cried. "Three digits. Two ways to change each digit—up or down. Three times two is six."

George laughed. "Very good, Charlie. You're no dummy." He looked stricken. "Ooops, no offense."

"No offense taken," Charlie said. "But we don't know which digit Edgar changed," he added.

"Right, Charlie," Pat said. "We'll just try to undo what he did when he locked the case."

George couldn't resist. "That's an example of a 'reversible operation,' Charlie." Charlie seemed less than thrilled with that bit of mathematical trivia. He stared at George with the same expression as Edgar.

"If our hypothesis is correct, two of these digits are part of the combination. Only one has changed," Pat said.

"Hypothesis—that's a guess, right?" Charlie asked.

Pat nodded. She moved the first cylinder up to 7 and tried to open the case. It remained locked. She moved it to 5. No luck. Pat returned it to 6 and tried the same procedure on the second cylinder.

As Pat worked, George pontificated. "What you're seeing is a problem-solving tool called trial and error . . ."

Charlie stared at George. "Uh huh . . ." He inched away from George and peered over Pat's shoulder. "The first two cyclinders didn't work? That would mean the third digit has to be the one Edgar changed, right?"

"Right, Charlie," Pat said. She could swear she felt the dummy breathing down her neck.

But they all held their breath as Pat moved the third cylinder to 7. The latch clicked open. Everyone smiled, except Edgar who was still staring stupidly into space.

George opened the case. Then, like Edgar before him, he slammed it shut. Pat and Charlie gaped at him.

"Boy, are you going to be sorry, Charlie," George said.

"Sorry about what?" Charlie asked.

"Sorry this isn't your case." George opened the case again and turned it around slowly so they could see inside.

The suitcase was filled with stacks and stacks and stacks of neatly bundled, crisp hundred-dollar bills.

DUM DE DUM DUM

CHAPTER

2

"Wow!" Pat said, stunned.

"I wish I'd said that," said Charlie.

George picked up a bundle of bills and riffled through it. "I'll bet there's a million bucks here."

"Want to go to lunch?" Charlie suggested. "My treat."

Pat came out of her trance. "If Edgar was shocked, wait until the other guy opens *his* suitcase."

"What do you mean?" George asked.

"George, if you had a suitcase with a million bucks in it and got home to find that it had been switched for a dummy named Lolly . . ."

"I see what you mean," George answered.

Pat looked around for a phone. "I'm going to call the airline. What airline were you on, Charlie?"

"Hey, from where I ride, they all look the same."

George looked at the tags on the case. He picked out the one that looked most recent. "TWM," he read. "Trans World Merge. Flight thirteen." Pat began dialing.

"Why are you calling the airline, Ms. Tuesday?" Charlie asked curiously.

"Bags get switched at airports all the time," Pat told

the dummy. "When people lose their bags, they can call. Usually the lost bag can be traced." A squawk in Pat's ear got her attention. "Hello. Baggage Claim, please . . ."

While Pat was on the phone, Charlie and George stared at the money. "I guess if I'd lost a million bucks on an airplane, I'd check it out," Charlie said.

George nodded. "We'll find out the name of the other traveler and just switch the bags back."

"Know what I'm going to say to Lolly when she gets home?" Charlie asked, a wicked gleam in his marble eye.

"What?"

"Lolly, you look like a million bucks!"

George slapped his leg and guffawed. When Pat turned from the telephone, George calmed down enough to ask, "What's the name, Pat?"

"Strange . . ." Pat looked puzzled.

"Strange who?" George prompted.

"No, not somebody named Strange," Pat sighed. "I mean something's strange. No one has called." She looked at Charlie. "When did you get in, Charlie?"

"Last night."

"Maybe the other guy hasn't missed his bag yet," George suggested.

"Maybe." Pat allowed. "But if you had a million bucks in your bag, wouldn't you check it right away?"

"I don't know," George shrugged. "Martha handles all that kind of stuff."

Pat rolled her eyes. "Anyway, I arranged to have the airport call Mathnet if anyone asks about a missing case.

"If it's okay with you two, we'll take this money to Mathnet for safekeeping. Here's a receipt." Pat held the slip out to Edgar. He stared right through her. She passed it to Charlie. The dummy's wooden hand lay limply at his side. Sighing, Pat placed the receipt on the table.

"We'll stay on this, Charlie," George was saying. "As soon as that other guy calls, we'll let you know and arrange to make the switch and get Lolly back."

Charlie looked sadly over at Edgar, who was staring at the ceiling. "Thanks, Mathnetters. I really appreciate your help. And so would Edgar . . . if he could."

Pat thought she noticed a tear in Charlie's eye. "I'm sure Edgar will snap out of it as soon as Lolly is back in the fold," she said quickly.

"I sure hope so," Charlie said, brightening. "He's due to spray me."

"Spray you?" George asked.

"Yeah. My family has a history of Dutch Elm disease." Pat winced.

* * *

The next day, Pat got to Mathnet HQ early and called Trans World Merge. George came in, carrying the familiar suitcase. He opened it and Pat looked inside. The case was empty. Pat hung up the phone.

"Well, it didn't take you long to spend the money," she teased.

George smiled. "Sergeant Abruzzi put it under lock and key in the police property room. It'll be safe there."

Pat updated her partner. "I just talked to TWM. It's been more than twenty-four hours now and no one has called about the missing suitcase. That's very unusual."

George scratched his head in thought, then examined

the case for clues about its owner. "Look at all these baggage checks. This bag has done some traveling."

That gave George an idea. "Hey, maybe this bag wasn't supposed to be off-loaded in New York," he said.

"What do you mean?"

"Sometimes planes have to make stops at other airports before reaching their final destinations," George explained. "They stop for fuel or to load and unload passengers. Maybe the plane this case was on flew off to another destination after it stopped here."

Pat nodded. "And the owner went with it, but the bag didn't." She reached for the phone. "Let's check with TWM."

* * *

The TWM airline operator asked the detectives to come to the airport in person so that an airline official could confirm the detectives' IDs.

"Goody, a trip to LaGuardia," George said when Pat filled him in.

The Mathnetters called Benny Pill, their undercover cop colleague, for transportation. It was a long ride out to the airport in Benny's undercover cab.

When George and Pat finally arrived at the airport they got in line at the TWM check-in counter. The attendant was dealing with a man in front of them.

"Enjoy your trip to Spokane, Washington, Mr. Crabbe," the attendant said. She smiled the smile she'd learned at TWM training school. "By the way, your flight is delayed. . . . Have a nice day!"

She stamped his ticket and Mr. Crabbe stamped off. It was the Mathnetters' turn to be served. The attendant smiled sweetly. "Hello, and where are we flying today?"

"Nowhere," George said.

"Then you've come to the right airline," the attendant said brightly.

George flashed his badge. "We're from Mathnet. We've got some questions about baggage handling . . ."

"I'm sorry, I can't help you." The woman's smile turned sad. "My job is to check people in and tell them their flights have been delayed. But perhaps my supervisor, Mr. Singletary, could help you."

Mr. Singletary could. He waved toward a door behind the counter. "Won't you step into my office?"

Singletary's office was spacious and comfortable, dominated by a large map of the United States behind his desk. The map showed all of the cities in the country served by TWM, with lines indicating connections. There were several airliner models around the office and a computer displaying that day's list of TWM flights.

Mr. Singletary leaned across his desk and stared at them intently. "Now, how may I be of service?"

George started. "Well, sir, with all the flights you have to all the cities you serve, how do the bags ever get to where they're supposed to go?"

Singletary beamed. He gestured toward his map. "This map shows every major airport in the United States and Canada. Each airport has a three-letter code. There are twenty-six letters in the alphabet. . . ." Singletary peered up at the ceiling. "Let's see, that's twenty-six to the third power, or 17,576 different combinations."

George was amazed. "Wow, did you work that out in your head?"

"No, it comes up all the time at parties," Singletary responded, proud to have impressed a mathematician.

Pat steered them back to business. "We're interested in the New York airport."

George interjected, "The New York area has three major airports, Pat."

Singletary pointed to New York on his map. "That's right. Kennedy Airport's code is JFK, LaGuardia is LGA, Newark is EWR. If you were flying to JFK from, say . . ."

"Los Angeles, California," George volunteered.

Singletary nodded. "All right, that's LAX."

George whispered to Pat, "I used to live there."

"I know, George."

Singletary continued. "You check your bags in Los Angeles and get a luggage tag. JFK is printed on the tag. Your luggage tag has a number that matches a claim check that's attached to your plane ticket."

"Then how do bags get switched?" Pat asked.

George took a guess. "People don't take time to match the number on their checks to tags on their cases."

"Right, Mr. Frankly. And lots of bags look alike. Mix-ups can occur."

Pat showed Singletary the baggage check from Edgar's bag. "Sir, can you look at this tag and tell us where it was supposed to be off-loaded?"

Singletary consulted his computer and struck a few keys. "That tag was for Flight 13, direct from Columbus, Ohio, to LaGuardia Airport, where it terminated."

Pat nodded. "So, whoever this bag belongs to *had* to have gotten off in New York."

Singletary said, "That's right."

Pat and George thanked him, and headed out of the terminal and back to Mathnet HQ.

* * *

Later, George was looking at a chart on his desk as Pat finished up a phone call. "Nothing about a bag from Flight 13? Okay, thank you." She hung up. "George, I don't get it. Why doesn't someone call the airline about the money?"

"Beats me." But George was smiling. "We do have one clue, though."

"Oh, what's that?" Pat asked, smiling back at her partner's proud expression.

"We know the places this bag has been." George held up a handful of baggage claim tags. "And look at this chart." He pointed to dots on the chart. Each was labeled with the name of a city. "According to the claim checks that were on the mystery bag, it flew each of these cities once: Cincinnati, Toledo, and Columbus—all in Ohio; Chicago, Illinois; Rochester, Minnesota; Cedar Rapids, Iowa; and New York City."

"What do the lines represent?" Pat asked.

George explained. "They show the only direct connections between cities. I think we can trace the bag's owner if we can figure out which flights it was on and check passenger lists for a name that's on all of them." George rubbed his chin. "The problem is that except for the last trip from Columbus to New York, all the other flight numbers are missing from the tags."

"I see." Pat nodded. "So we know the bag went to these cities, but we don't know in what order."

George added some arrows to his chart. They indicated a circular path around the points. "Here's one way it could have gone."

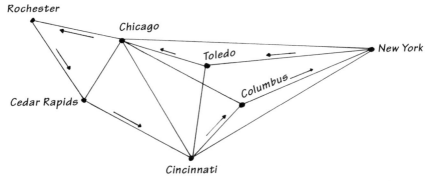

Rochester
Chicago
Toledo
New York
Cedar Rapids
Columbus
Cincinnati

Pat looked at the chart and her eyes lit up. "George! That's a Hamiltonian circuit. I did a paper on them at Mathnet U. I'm crazy about Hamiltonian circuits!"

"Then you know a circuit shows a path around a graph that visits each point once and only once, then returns to the beginning."

Pat nodded excitedly. "Each segment of the path is called an edge, George, and no edge is used twice." Pat frowned. "But this graph shows only one possible path the suitcase could take. Aren't there others?"

"Let's check," George suggested.

"Okay. We'll assume the trip started in New York. Since the case ended up here, it may be the owner's home base," Pat said. "So it couldn't have gone to Columbus as the first stop."

"Why not?"

"Because the suitcase arrived at its last stop, New York, *from* Columbus. We can only stop at each city once. If Columbus is the fifth stop, it can't be the second one, too."

"Right." George quickly drew a clean chart on the blackboard. Then he marked a new circuit. "How about this? . . . New York to Chicago to Rochester to Cedar Rapids to Cincinnati to Columbus to New York."

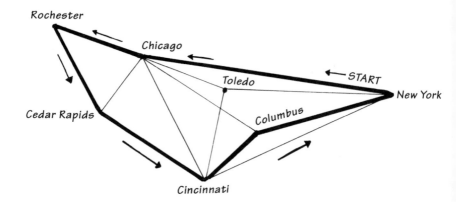

Pat squinted at the chart and shook her head. "N.G."

"No good," George agreed. "I left out Toledo." He squinted at the chart too, then snapped his fingers. "I think I've got it." He began drawing a new path.

"New York to Toledo to Cincinnati to Cedar Rapids to Rochester to Chicago to Columbus to New York."

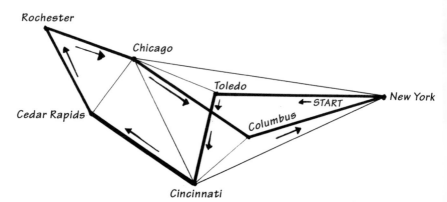

"That works!" Pat exclaimed. The Mathnetters tinkered with the graph some more but found no other paths that worked. "So we know two ways the suitcase could have made the circuit," Pat concluded. "But it still doesn't explain why its owner hasn't called about the case."

"You know, Pat," George mused, "maybe the guy who owns the bag can't call."

"What do you mean? He can't find a phone?"

"No, Pat." George lowered his voice dramatically. "But what if the money is *illegal*? What if it's illegal gambling money or stolen money?" George's eyes gleamed.

"I see." Pat looked thoughtful. "He'd be afraid to call the airline. But he knows another traveler has the money, and he'll want it back."

The Mathnet duo pondered for a moment; then a light bulb went off for Pat. "When he finds Lolly, he'll guess the other owner is a ventriloquist. That means Charlie and Edgar could be in danger."

"But they don't have the money."

"I know that and you know that," Pat said. "But the *owner* doesn't know that."

George grabbed the phone. "I'll call Charlie. Get Benny. We've got to get over there fast!"

Pat ran out in search of Benny as George dialed Edgar's number. Someone picked up the phone and breathed heavily into the receiver. "Edgar?" There was no answer. "Charlie?" Still no answer.

George gulped. He hoped that the person on the other end was Edgar, and that the ventriloquist could still hear in his odd state. George spoke urgently into the phone. "This is George Frankly, Mathnet. Someone may be after you and the money. Lock your doors and open them for no one. We're on our way."

Benny Pill's undercover cab got to The Broken Arms apartment complex in three minutes flat. George and Pat rushed down the hall and took up positions on either side of the door. George pounded on the door. "Charlie, it's . . ."

KABOOM!!!

There was a gigantic explosion. The door burst open and smoke flooded the hallway.

DUM DE DUM DUM

CHAPTER
3

The door was hanging on broken hinges, so the Mathnetters just pushed through and into the apartment. Through the cloud of smoke they found that the furniture near the door lay tumbled and broken on the floor from the force of the explosion.

"Are you all right, Charlie?" Pat called. Then, as an afterthought, "Edgar? Are you okay?"

Choking and coughing, they waved away the last of the smoke. Through its clearing vapors they saw Charlie and Edgar. The dummy was holding a blunderbuss pointed at the door. Protruding from the gun's muzzle was a flag that said "BANG!"

"I'll mow you down . . . stay away . . . stay away or I'll moider youse . . ." Charlie was muttering, in a daze.

"Stop that!" Pat said sternly as George grabbed the gun. "Charlie, it's me, Pat. And George."

"Sorry. Sorry, Pat." Charlie blinked. He began to settle down. "It's just that when George called it put me a bit on edge . . ."

"A bit?" George said, looking at the gun. "Wars have been won with less firepower."

Pat looked behind Charlie and spotted Edgar. He was staring at a lamp, as vacant as ever. She shrugged and began helping George pick up the debris. Pat spotted the phone. Its receiver was missing.

"Charlie, you're going to have to stay on guard. The person who has Lolly may be a crook. He may try to get in touch with you." She looked at the broken phone. "Although that might be a bit harder now."

"He may be looking for you to get his money back," George added.

"But we haven't got the money," Charlie said. "Besides, how's he going to find us?"

"Well, he's got Lolly, so he has to know that he's looking for a ventriloquist," George pointed out.

Charlie nodded. "Good point. If he knows that, it would easy to trace Lolly back to Edgar."

Pat asked, "Just how would he do that?"

"Ventriloquist dummy makers," said Charlie.

"We'll check around to see if anyone's been checking around." George picked up an 8-by-10 glossy photo of Edgar, Charlie and Lolly that was lying among the debris. "Mind if we take this?"

"Be my guest," Charlie said. "Hey, you know where else this guy might check?"

"Where?" Pat and George both asked.

"With show business agents . . . the people who get jobs for us."

Pat nodded. "Do you have an agent?"

"One of the best. Her name is . . . Broadway Annie Rose."

Pat said, "Thanks, Charlie. We're on our way." Pat

24

took one look back at Edgar. She thought maybe he winked, then thought better of it as she and George headed out of the apartment.

*   *   *

In Benny Pill's undercover cab, George asked Benny to check out the dummy makers while they were talking to Charlie and Edgar's agent. Benny dropped George and Pat off in front of a shabby office building. Its appearance prepared them for the creaky, bumpy elevator ride to the third floor, but nothing could have prepared them for the sights and sounds of the office they entered. Crowded inside were foot jugglers, magicians, a man with a trained goat, a man

eating bowling balls, a lady who sang opera while scrambling yak eggs, and a seal that did not seem to be either trained or housebroken. Pat and George made their way through the melange to the receptionist. A nameplate on her desk identified her as Miss Jessica.

"Welcome to the office of Broadway Annie Rose," Miss Jessica greeted them. "What do you do?"

Pat said, "I beg your pardon?"

"What is your show business specialty?" Jessica asked. "Juggling, singing, trained animals, imitations . . .?"

George and Pat both showed their badges and said in unison, "Mathnet."

"Oh? We don't get much call for Mathnet." Miss Jessica looked curious. "Ever do math *without* a net?"

"You misunderstand," Pat said. "We're *with* Mathnet and we're here to see . . ."

With that, an inner door burst open and a large woman with dyed red hair appeared, wearing a mismatched jacket and pants outfit. She flung her arms skyward and belted out, "Broadway Annie Rooooooose!"

George took one step back. Trying to set an example, he spoke quietly. "Are you Annie?"

Annie sang, loudly: "The sun will come out tomorroooooow . . ."

Annie beckoned them into her office as she sang. George and Pat looked at one another, shrugged, and entered. The office was cluttered with costumes and props, and the walls were filled with photos of Annie posing with everybody from a stripper to a president.

"Thank you for seeing us, Broadway Annie," Pat began.

"Likewise, I'm sure. What can I do for you?"

"We'd like to ask you about one of your clients," George said.

Pat added, "Three of them, actually. Charlie, Edgar and Lolly."

Annie smiled. "Great act. Wanna book 'em?"

"No, you see . . ."

"Anything wrong?" Annie interrupted Pat.

"Yes, Annie," George said. "Lolly has been kidnapped."

"That's terrible," Annie said grimly. Her smile disappeared. "Any suspects?"

"Not yet," George said, "but we were wondering if anybody has been asking about them."

"Nope. They just finished a tour I booked for them."

"You're their agent, right?" Pat asked.

"Right." Annie smoothed her red hair with matching red fingernails. "I'm their ten-percenter."

George was puzzled. "Ten-percenter?"

"That's right. Agents are called ten-percenters because we get ten percent of the money our clients receive."

"That doesn't seem fair," Pat said.

"Do my ears detect sass?" Annie queried.

"No, but . . ."

"We agents are entitled to at least that much for getting them their gigs and putting up with some of these *artistes*," Annie said. Thinking of the seal, Pat and George had to agree.

"We not only find them jobs," Annie continued, "but we also have to schedule their travel. And that ain't easy." Annie searched through the rubble on her desk and found a scrap of paper. She handed it to Pat. "Here's the schedule for Edgar's latest tour."

Pat scanned the list. "So first you sent them from New York to Detroit . . ."

"They performed in Detroit, Michigan?" George said, peering over Pat's shoulder. "That's a great town."

"No, Mr. Frankly." Annie shook her red head. "The act was actually booked into a little town outside Detroit. A place called Ann Arbor."

Pat looked at the itinerary. "That's right. It says here Edgar drove from Detroit to Ann Arbor, then back to Detroit again."

"When an act can't fly into one of those little burgs, I send them to the nearest airport, wherever that is."

"Next, they played in Middletown, Ohio," Pat noted. "Let me guess, no flights to Middletown, right?"

"You got it," Annie pointed a finger at Pat and nodded cheerfully. "So I routed them to Dayton, and they rented a car and drove to Middletown. Then they flew on to Des Moines, Iowa; Minneapolis, Minnesota; and Columbus, Ohio. Then, according to the schedule, back to New York."

"Just out of curiosity, how much money did they make for this tour?" George asked.

"$75,000."

George whistled. "So you made ten percent of $75,000?"

"That's right. $7,500." Annie looked pleased.

"You've got a nice business," Pat commented.

"It's not always big bucks, lady, let me tell you." Annie sighed. "Did you see that foot juggler out front?"

"Uh-huh," Pat said.

"You didn't shake with him, did you?"

"No, why?"

"The last guy who did got athlete's hand." Annie swung her feet up on the desk. "Anyway, that foot juggler out there hasn't had a job since I booked him for a podiatrists' luncheon in Soho. It paid forty-seven fifty."

"Four thousand seven hundred fifty dollars?" George wondered, looking in awe at Annie's feet. She was wearing a pair of glittery gold spike-heeled sandals.

Annie shook her head. "Forty-seven dollars and fifty cents. Hardly covered the athlete's foot spray."

"I take it back, Annie." Pat smiled. "You do earn your ten percent."

"You can bet your sweet smile on it, Toots."

Pat handed Annie a business card. "If anyone inquires about Charlie and Edgar . . ."

Annie smiled. "I'll give you a blast on the horn."

"You can just call us on the phone if it's easier," George said as the Mathnetters left.

Annie gave him a look, but smiled as she sang, "So looooooong!"

* * *

Back at Mathnet Headquarters, George headed for the phone. Pat headed for the property room. She came back loaded with money just as George hung up.

"I called Benny," George reported. "So far no one has contacted any dummy makers, but they'll call if anyone does."

George watched Pat as she sorted through the stacks of bills she was carrying. "What are you doing with the money, Pard?"

Pat held up a report. "They counted it."

"How much?"

"One million bucks—exactly."

"Tidy little sum."

Pat looked upset. "There's something else, though. Something that makes it look like Charlie and Edgar know more about this than they'll admit."

"That's crazy, Pat." George was shocked.

"But George, look at this. The money comes from several different cities." Pat showed George how each stack was wrapped in a sleeve with the name and location of a bank stamped on it.

"So?"

Pat indicated some of the stacks. "This one is from the Bank of Columbus. Here's a bunch from the Des Moines Trust . . . the Ann Arbor Savings . . ."

"Money comes from different banks, Pat. That's not unusual."

"No, it isn't," Pat agreed, "but the rest of this money comes from Minneapolis and Middletown."

"Five cities." George shrugged. "So what?"

"But George, those are the *same* five cities that were just visited by our friends . . ."

With a grim look on his face, George reluctantly finished, ". . . Charlie, Edgar and Lolly."

DUM DE DUM DUM

CHAPTER
4

Pat overslept the next morning, so she took a cab instead of the subway. It was the day of the annual "Spring Is Almost Here Tulip Festival." Streets were blocked off and it took forever to get to HQ. When Pat finally entered, George and Captain Grecco were there, looking at a chart.

As she hung up her jacket, Pat asked, "What's up, guys? What's the chart?"

Grecco answered. "When I learned of the 'coincidence' of the five cities, I called the police in each one."

"Remember my theory that the money might be illegal?" George said. "We wanted to see if there had been any robberies in those cities."

Pat took one look at her partner's unhappy expression and feared the worst. "I take it there were?"

"A few, Pat." George confirmed the worst.

Pat looked carefully at the columns on the chalkboard. George had listed each city that Edgar's act had been scheduled to visit. Written underneath each city was the amount of money missing in the robberies.

"In Ann Arbor, a bank was robbed." Grecco pointed to the chart. "They got $325,000."

Pat looked at another location. "There was a $131 bank robbery in Columbus, Ohio?" she asked. "Pretty piddly."

George answered, "It wasn't a bank. Thieves robbed the Honors Scholarship Fund at Ohio State."

Pat tried to find a bright side. "At least they didn't get much."

"Didn't get much? Wiped it out, that's all."

Grecco pointed to the chart again. "In Des Moines they knocked over an armored car for $310,000."

Pat asked, "What about Middletown?"

"A shopping mall. They got $250,171."

"And Minneapolis?"

"Another bank, for $400,000." Grecco answered. "Total take . . . $1,285,302."

Pat scratched her head. "So, if what we have is the stolen money, we're short nearly 300 grand. Are you going to bring Charlie and Edgar in for questioning?"

"I've sent their pictures to the various police departments to see if they can be positively identified," Grecco said. "Things don't look very good for them."

"Captain, I know they didn't do it," Pat pleaded.

"Me, too," George added.

Grecco shrugged. "I hope you're right, Mathnetters."

The phone buzz interrupted them and Pat answered. "Tuesday. Oh, yes. Right away." She hung up and turned to George. "DA Wofford wants to see us."

"The District Attorney?"

Grecco jumped in. "She may have gotten the ID reports. She can be a real bulldog," he warned.

"Should we talk to her or just bark?" George wondered nervously as he and Pat headed for the door.

* * *

George and Pat were a bit anxious as they headed to the DA's office. Her reputation was well known, but the Mathnetters had never had to deal with her. The DA was pacing when they entered her poshly furnished office. She looked angry.

Pat cleared her throat. "You wanted to see us?"

The DA nodded and gestured toward a sofa. "Yes, have a seat."

George patted the sofa as he sat down. "Boy, DA's sure have spiffier offices than mathematicians."

The DA stared at George.

"We don't even *have* a couch," George continued.

"I didn't ask you up here to admire my couch," the DA growled. "I understand that you two have become friendly with the guilty parties in this matter."

Pat was incredulous. "Guilty parties?"

DA Wofford picked up a file. "The robbers . . . Edgar Bergman and Charlie McShtick."

"Well, I must have missed the trial when they were found guilty of robbery." George was getting angry.

"The trial, in this case, Mr. Frankly, is a formality."

"What do you mean?" Pat demanded to know.

"They were identified in the holdups in . . ." The DA dropped reports on her desk one by one. "Ann Arbor . . .

Middletown . . . Des Moines . . . Minneapolis . . . and Columbus. Positive ID. And we caught 'em with the money."

Pat jumped in. "They *surrendered* the money."

"Don't be a nitpicker, Ms. Tuesday."

George reached out. "May I see the reports?"

"No," the DA said, pulling the file back. "Take my word for it. They were identified."

There was a very quiet pause in the room until Pat asked, "What are you going to do?"

"Do? Nothing." The DA looked pleased with herself. "I've already done it. Your buddies are in New York's finest jail. Just thought you'd like to know."

After a stunned instant, Pat and George leaped up and rushed for the door.

"Softies," the DA hissed, by way of good-bye.

* * *

Pat and George returned to Mathnet HQ. They immediately called Benny to meet them with his undercover cab so they might visit Edgar and Charlie in jail. As they drove crosstown in the cab, they griped about the DA.

"That Wofford is one tough bird," Pat said.

"She sure is," George agreed. "Do you know her, Benny?"

"DA Wofford? Yeah, I know her." Benny looked like he wished he didn't. "She's looking to become governor of the state one day. Some say she might even go into presidential politics. She's very ambitious."

"I bet she'd put her own mother in jail," George said.

Benny laughed. "She did. Her mother's doing seven to ten for baking soggy cookies when the DA was a kid."

Benny braked in front of the jail.

"Good luck, guys," he said as Pat and George got out.

The Mathnetters entered the jail and were escorted toward the cell where Edgar and Charlie were being held. The jail was dank and cold. The "clunk" of each barred door echoed through the building and sent chills down the spines of the mathematicians. Both decided that jail was definitely not a place to be.

"Charlie and Edgar must be mortified," Pat whispered.

George agreed. "Jail knocks the starch out of people."

The guard stopped and gestured toward a cell. Then he stepped back to allow Pat and George a bit of privacy.

"Let me out of here, you dirty rats," said a familiar squeaky voice. "I'm innocent, innocent, I tell you. I'm too young to die. I wanna see the sunrise again. I wanna stop and smell the roses. I wanna feel the wind blow through my knotholes . . ."

George tried to stop the flow. "Easy, Charlie . . ."

"Get me a mouthpiece, get me a rewrite, get me a ham sandwich . . . hold the mayo . . ."

Pat finally intervened. "Charlie, calm down!"

Charlie's wooden schnozz poked between two of the bars. "Pat! George! Sorry, I didn't know it was you. Jail always does this to me."

"Have you been in jail before?" George asked.

"No, but I've seen a lot of bad prison movies." The dummy started to smile. "Hey, George, did you ever see *Life Was a Song, But He Lived in Sing Sing?*"

Pat sighed. Charlie was back in form. "Charlie, this is serious," she said. "Do you swear that you and Edgar did

not commit those robberies?"

They all looked at Edgar. He was wearing the same striped prison uniform Charlie wore and staring blankly at the cell's iron bars. Except for the clothes, jail hadn't changed Edgar one bit.

Charlie looked back at Pat and George. "I can speak for Edgar. We absolutely did not steal that money. Those cops are barking up the wrong tree."

George said, "But they have witnesses in Ann Arbor, Minneapolis, Des Moines, Middletown, and Columbus who will swear you did."

Charlie's face brightened. "Wait a minute. Did you say Minneapolis?"

"Yes," Pat said. "Why?"

"Because we weren't even *in* Minneapolis." Charlie was bouncing in excitement.

George shook his head. "Come off it, Charlie. Broadway Annie Rose said she booked you there."

"She did. But we didn't do the show."

"Why not?" Pat asked.

"We couldn't get there." Charlie smiled in triumph. "There was a terrible blizzard in Minneapolis."

Pat looked confused. "So where were you when you were supposed to be in Minneapolis, Charlie?"

"We were in the airport in Des Moines." Charlie sounded sure of his facts. "We finally just flew on to our next show in Columbus, Ohio."

Pat and George looked at each other. They believed Charlie.

"Okay, pal," George said as the Mathnetters turned to leave. "We've got some work to do."

"We'll be in touch," Pat encouraged.

"Thanks," Charlie said. "You know where we'll be."

* * *

Both Pat and George arrived at Mathnet HQ early the next day. They busied themselves on their phones. Pat asked Captain Grecco to check on whether or not the act had performed in Minneapolis, then checked with other witnesses. George was trying to track down the itinerary of the suitcase. They hung up at the same time.

"The witnesses all describe a man in a top hat and silk scarf with a dummy. Both wore masks," Pat said. "It sure sounds like a description of Charlie and Edgar."

"Yes, Pat, but if Charlie's right, then one witness at least is wrong. The one in Minneapolis."

"Because they weren't there," Pat finished.

"Benny's checking who else the robber might be," George said. "Have you called the airline recently?"

"Yes, George. No one has inquired about the bag."

Captain Grecco entered at that moment, carrying a chart under his arm.

"Hi, Captain Grecco," Pat greeted him. "Did you talk with the promoter in Minneapolis?"

"Sure did, Pat. And Charlie told the truth. They couldn't get there because of the weather." Grecco's smile lit up his face. "I got them out of jail."

Pat smiled back. "Great. Thanks, Captain Grecco."

"What's the chart?" George asked.

"I've graphed Charlie and Edgar's original itinerary, George." Grecco rolled out his chart on a desk.

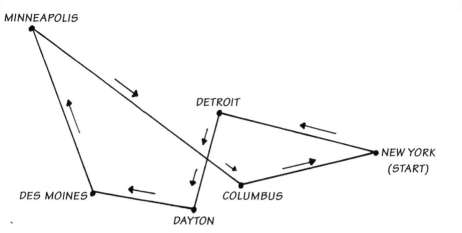

The Mathnetters bent over for a look. Pat was elated. "Skipper! You made a Hamiltonian circuit. I love them!"

"Yeah," Grecco shyly answered. "Me too. I make 'em every chance I get." He pointed to his chart. "Edgar's act was scheduled to go from New York to Detroit to Dayton to Des Moines to Minneapolis to Columbus and then back to New York."

George jumped in. "Just a darn minute. Look at this!" He grabbed one of his own charts plotting the case's path.

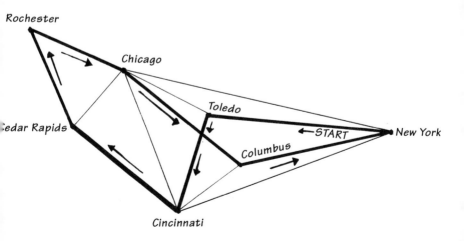

"These two Hamiltonian circuits are almost the same shape!" George traced the paths.

"I'll be hornswoggled. You're right!" Grecco cheered.

"Good work, Captain," George said. "The bag could have been following Charlie and Edgar. We were going to ask the airlines to pull passenger lists on those routes. We'd better get on that right away. Maybe a passenger from the Columbus to New York flight will show up on other flights in the circuit."

"You follow that angle. I've got people checking whether there were other ventriloquists doing shows in those areas," Grecco told them. "I'll be right back."

"Thanks, Captain," Pat smiled.

"*De nada*," Grecco said as he headed for the door. He was nearly bowled over by an angry DA.

"Tuesday, Frankly. What are you doing to my case?" she asked furiously.

"What do you mean?" Pat said sweetly.

"Those two crooks got out on some technicality."

"It wasn't a technicality. It was a solid alibi," George said. He tried to be diplomatic. "We didn't want to see you involved in a miscarriage of justice."

"A miscarriage of *what*?" the DA asked. She stormed out, nearly running over Grecco again as he reentered the office with a file folder. "Out of my way!"

Grecco dusted himself off. "Charming example of the legal profession," he said, watching the DA go.

"Any luck, Skipper?" George asked.

"Not much, I'm afraid."

"No other ventriloquists?" Pat was surprised.

"Not many. There was one performing at a mall opening in Ypsilanti, a town near Ann Arbor. But that's all we've found so far. Here's a local newspaper review."

George flipped open the folder and glanced at the clipping inside. "Some act called Nosebleed and Snerd. Did they appear anywhere else on the route?"

"Not that we've found so far. Sorry."

"Thanks, Captain," Pat said.

This time when Grecco left he bumped into Charlie and Edgar. The dummy was a lot more polite than the DA. "Excuse me, Captain," he said.

George brightened at the sight of his friends. "Hey, you two . . ." Then he looked at Edgar. ". . . or you one. Good to see you." Edgar, still looking completely out of it, shuffled to a chair with Charlie.

"Thanks for helping me get out of that lockup, Mathnetters," Charlie said gratefully. "I owe you one."

"Maybe you could help *us*, Charlie," Pat said. "Ever hear of an act called Nosebleed and Snerd?"

Charlie thought for a minute. "No . . . well . . . maybe. There's a stirring in the sawdust of my mind. Edgar would probably know them."

Everyone looked at Edgar. Edgar looked at his shoelaces. Charlie seemed to shrug. "Why?" he asked.

Pat headed across the room for the phone. "Just a hunch. I'm going to call Broadway Annie."

"Any change in Edgar?" George asked Charlie.

"Not really," Charlie said. "But this morning when I was drinking a glass of juice, I thought his lips moved."

"He'll come around," George said, patting Charlie on the back. "Charlie, if you didn't commit these robberies, you may have been set up."

"You mean someone wanted to make people think it was Edgar and me?"

"Exactly." George looked serious. "Who would have such a motive? Who are your enemies?"

"We don't have any. We are beloved." Charlie frowned and growled, "And the first slob who says we aren't gets a brogue in the slats."

"Calm down, Charlie," George said. "Think now. Who would stand to gain with you guys behind bars?"

"The other inmates," Charlie said. "We had those cons in stitches."

George pressed on. "You said you were going to do that big television show . . ."

"Yeah. It's tomorrow night. ASFAS."

George nodded. "The Award Show for the Award Shows. But with Lolly missing, you lost the job."

"Right," Charlie sniffed.

"Who got the gig, Charlie?"

"An act I never heard of. Merlin and the Munchkins."

Pat rejoined the duo, or trio, if you counted Edgar, which Pat didn't. "Guess what Annie said?"

"What?" George perked up at the prospect of some showbiz gossip.

"She said that Snerd hates Edgar and has for years."

Charlie was clearly startled. "Why?"

"Professional jealousy," George guessed. "He was jealous of the money and fame that Edgar had."

"That's about it," Pat confirmed. "Annie said that Nosebleed and Snerd are a terrible act."

"Does she represent them?" George asked.

"No. Annie said nobody will," Pat said. "They book all

their own gigs, anything from mall openings to birthday parties. They're a couple of loners."

The DA burst back into the room. At least this time Captain Grecco was safely in his office.

George spoke first. "Hello again, DA Wofford. How may we be of service to your career this time?"

"I thought you might like to know that about half of the stolen money is traceable," the DA smirked.

Pat's eyebrows shot up. "You mean the banks had records of the serial numbers?"

"Exactly." The DA smiled nastily at Charlie and Edgar. "So, we traced your million dollars . . ."

"And?" George interrupted. He didn't like the DA's gleeful expression.

"And none of the money matches!"

George frowned. "But if *half* the money was marked and they stole one million three hundred thousand . . ."

". . . then at least *some* of the money would have to match," Pat added. "Because we have more than half the amount here."

The DA smirked again. "Right. So we looked at the money a little more closely. The stuff's bogus!"

Charlie did a double take. "Bogus?"

Pat, George and the DA answered in unison, "Counterfeit."

The DA stared straight at Charlie, her nasty grin growing wider and wider. The dummy's wooden teeth began to chatter. The DA just laughed. "Ever been arrested for counterfeiting . . . Dummy?"

DUM DE DUM DUM

CHAPTER
5

DA Wofford didn't arrest Charlie and Edgar, but she warned them to stay in town. Pat and George knew it was only a matter of time until the DA built a case that would put their friends back under lock and key.

The next morning when Pat arrived at the office, George was on the phone. Pat began looking through the case file to get herself up to speed.

George hung up. "That was a street person, Pat."

"George, we have a million dollars of counterfeit money and robberies that amount to $1.3 million on our hands." Pat sounded exasperated. "Where'd the counterfeit money come from, where's the real missing money, and how is a 'street person' going to help?"

"He knows what's going on 'illegal-wise,' Pat," George explained. "His name is Blinky and he runs a shoeshine stand. Come on. Let's talk to him."

Pat shrugged, but put her jacket on and followed

George out the door and down the street to Blinky's stand.

Blinky was an old man, pudgy and bald. George introduced Pat and handed Blinky one of the suspect bills.

"Counterfeit," Blinky stated, after barely a glance. He started shining George's shoes.

"How can you tell?" Pat asked.

Blinky paused in his shoeshine to point to parts of the bill. "You look to make sure the picture is clear and distinct. Make sure the borders aren't blurred. Check the treasury seal to make sure it's clear."

Blinky handed the bill back to George. "I know this is fake because the serial numbers aren't evenly spaced."

George pocketed the bogus bill and asked, "Blinky, how does one get counterfeit loot?"

"You either print it or you pay for it, Mr. Frankly."

"You mean you can *buy* it?" Pat was amazed.

"Yep. Twenty points on the buck it usually costs. A point is a percentage point."

Pat was confused. "Twenty percent of what?"

Blinky was impatient. "Of the whole."

"So if I wanted to buy a counterfeit dollar bill," George proposed, "it would cost me . . ."

"Twenty percent of one dollar. Twenty cents."

"And if I wanted to buy a counterfeit *one-hundred*-dollar bill?" Pat asked.

"Twenty bucks, Ms. Tuesday. So you'd clear 80 dollars if you got away with passing it. But if you get caught with bogus bills, you do real time . . . in prison."

George was still concerned with the numbers. "So one million dollars of fake money would cost me . . ."

"Two hundred thousand dollars," Blinky said, finishing George's shoes with a dramatic snap of his cloth.

Pat said, "George, our man could have spent two hundred thousand dollars of the real, *stolen* money to buy one million dollar's worth of bogus bills."

"Right, Pat, and he'd still have over a million dollars of the robbery money left over."

George patted Blinky on the back. "Thanks a lot, Blinky. You've been very helpful."

"No prob. I love Mathnet." Blinky looked shyly down at his own scuffed brogues. "In fact, I want to be a mathematician when I grow up."

Pat looked at Blinky. "When you grow up?"

"I'm young at heart, Ms. Tuesday."

* * *

The phone was ringing as George and Pat entered the office. George answered it. "Frankly, Mathnet. Uh-huh, uh-huh. Wow! You're positive? Thank you very much." George hung up. He rooted around his desk and produced his graph of the mystery suitcase's trip.

"That was the airline, Pat," George informed her. "They've identified a name which is common to all the flights our mystery bag was on."

Pat noted her partner's excited face and was suitably curious. "What's the name, George?"

"Floyd Snerd!"

"Nosebleed and Snerd." Pat smiled in satisfaction. Then her smile faded. She pulled out the two charts—the one with the suitcases's stops and the one with Edgar's. "But George, Snerd went to different cities than Edgar did, and Edgar's stops were where the robberies occurred."

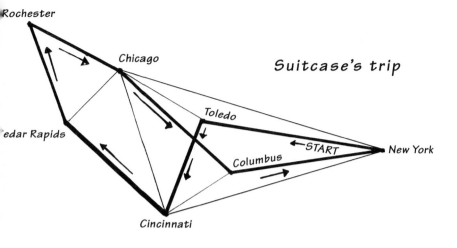

Suitcase's trip

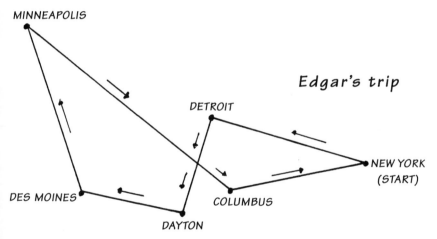

Edgar's trip

The Mathnetters compared the two charts. "Look, Pat. The first robbery was near Detroit. . . . Toledo is nearby. The second was near Dayton. . . . Cincinnati isn't far. Next is Des Moines, and Cedar Rapids is pretty close."

"Yes, but what about the next one?" Pat asked.

George sighed. "I see what you mean. Edgar couldn't

get to Minneapolis because of the weather, so neither could Snerd." Then he brightened. "But the airlines said Snerd flew from Cedar Rapids to *Rochester*. And his flight left earlier than Edgar's did."

"Snerd must have flown to Rochester before the weather turned bad," Pat concluded. "George, he could have rented a car and pulled the robbery."

"And Snerd would have no way of knowing that Edgar and Charlie's show in Minneapolis would be canceled."

Pat picked up her phone. "I'll check car rentals."

George picked up his phone. "And I'll see if I can get an address on our Mr. Snerd."

Just then, Captain Grecco came in with a scruffy-looking man in tow. George and Pat put down their phones.

Grecco pushed the man in, saying, "Folks, meet Ebeneezer Squeeze. Tell them what you do, Mr. Squeeze."

"I'm a landlord," the man muttered.

"Tell them why you're here, Mr. S.," Grecco barked.

"I was collecting my rent envelopes, doing my evictions, turning off the heat in some of my buildings . . ."

"Get on with it," Grecco ordered.

"Well, Captain, I was owed some back rent," Squeeze whined. "But when I got the dough and went to deposit it, the bank said it was hot money."

Grecco waved the bills in the air. "These are five one-hundred-dollar bills from the armored car robbery in Des Moines."

"Where did you get them, Mr. Squeeze?" Pat asked.

"A tenant." Squeeze spat the name. "Floyd Snerd."

George grabbed a pencil. "What's the address?"

"It's 1313 Thirteenth Place."

George wrote down the address. "Thank you for helping us catch a despicable villain."

Squeeze shook his mangy head. "It won't do you any good. Snerd packed up lock, stock, and dummy and left this morning. He said he was going to Costa Rica."

George and Pat were crestfallen. They sank limply into their chairs as Grecco marched Squeeze out the door.

After a moment, Charlie and Edgar walked in, both dressed in tuxedos.

George perked up a bit. "Hello, Charlie. Any change in Edgar?"

Charlie turned to look at the stuporous ventriloquist. "No. I'm afraid he's still out there."

"Unfortunately," George said, "so is Snerd."

"We found the solution to the problem, but we found it too late," Pat said. "Well, maybe the Costa Rican authorities will find Snerd and send him back for trial."

"Knock on wood," George said, tapping Charlie's noggin. Pat thought maybe he should knock instead on Edgar, who was looking especially wooden in his tuxedo.

"My guess is," George was saying, "with more than a million dollars, Snerd can change his appearance and live the life of Riley."

"Really?" Charlie said.

George laughed. "By the way, Charlie, why are you both wearing monkey suits?"

Charlie looked down at his tuxedo. "Actually, we dropped by to see if you wanted to go to ASFAS."

"ASFAS?" George and Pat said.

"The Award Show for the Award Shows," Charlie reminded them. "I'd better hurry. It's already started."

Pat shook her head. "Maybe some other time, Charlie. Thanks anyway."

"Okay. I want to catch the act who's subbing for us. It's a ventriloquist with a magic act." Charlie tried to sound cheerful. "I heard Merlin cuts one of the Munchkins in half for the finale. It should be good for a laugh. See ya."

As the door closed, the phone rang. George answered it briskly. "Mathnet, Frankly. Oh, hi, Annie." Pat looked up and listened to George's end of the conversation with interest. "Uh-huh. No one has? Are you sure? That's strange. Well, thanks for your help. What? Oh, sure, we'll call if we need some entertainment for the Policeman's Ball. 'Bye."

George turned to Pat. "Broadway Annie says that no one's ever heard of Merlin and the Munchkins."

George and Pat slumped back into their chairs. Then Pat's eyebrows shot up. Her face brightened. Another light bulb had gone off in her head.

"George, how did ASFAS find out so fast that Lolly was missing, and that the act needed to be replaced?"

George thought back to that first meeting with Charlie. Then he shrugged. "I don't think Charlie mentioned it. He just said they were informed."

Pat looked for a number, then reached for the phone. "How could they be?" Pat asked as she dialed the number. "Charlie didn't tell them, and Edgar has been in a trance since he found out Lolly was missing."

"Who are you calling, Pat?"

Pat ignored him for a moment and turned to the

phone. "Hello, ASFAS? I'm Pat Tuesday with Mathnet. You're sponsoring the show tonight which was going to feature Charlie, Edgar, and Lolly, right?" She nodded to herself. "I wonder if you could tell me why you canceled them?" Pat looked surprised. "I see. Okay. Yes, thank you." Pat recited their fax number and hung up. "George, she said ASFAS received a letter. She's faxing us a copy."

George was puzzled. "Pat, we're not on the same page."

"Something doesn't add up, George. The ASFAS producer said she got a letter from Edgar."

"So? He probably wrote it after the trip."

"You saw Edgar. Did he really look like someone who could write his own name, let alone a letter?" Pat asked. The fax machine made its distinctive "ding," and Pat scurried to get the letter. "Listen to this, George. 'Dear ASFAS, We will be unable to host your upcoming show because Lolly is missing. Please be advised, as a substitute, I highly recommend Merlin and the Munchkins, a delightful ventriloquist and magic act. Sorry for the inconvenience. Sincerely, Edgar Bergman.'" Pat looked up from the page. "According to the date, this letter was written *last week.*"

George was puzzled. "But Edgar didn't know Lolly was going to be missing then."

"Exactly, George. And guess where the letter was mailed from." Pat eyed her partner. "Rochester, Minnesota."

"Edgar wasn't even *in* Rochester . . ." George had finally caught on.

Together, the Mathnetters said, ". . . but Snerd was."

"George, Snerd could have set the whole thing up." Pat began pacing excitedly while she figured it out. "He could have robbed the stores, disguised as Edgar and Charlie, and kept the real money to retire on."

George joined Pat in her pacing. "And he used the counterfeit money to frame Edgar, a man he has hated for years. And the thing is, he got away with it."

"Maybe not, Pard. Clearly, jealousy is behind everything Snerd has done. He wouldn't miss one last shot at one-upping Edgar. We've got to get to the awards show—" Pat couldn't resist—"ASFAS as we can!"

They rushed across town. Half an hour later they were at the posh New York Academy of Awards, where the ceremony was taking place. Pat and George quietly entered the back of the ballroom and scanned the stage.

"And lastly, let me say, I deserve this award and you don't," a tuxedoed recipient was saying. There was a murmur through the elegantly dressed audience. Pat and George got the feeling the show had not been going well.

They spotted Charlie and Edgar at a table nearby. As they sat down at the table, Pat whispered to Charlie, "We changed our minds. How's Merlin?"

"He's awful, Pat . . . just awful." Charlie hung his wooden head. "Makes one ashamed to be in this business we call 'show.'" Pat glanced at Edgar, who remained impervious to the goings-on.

Meanwhile, another man swept onstage, ushering off the award-winner. This second man also wore a tuxedo, but he sported a top hat and a cape as well. It was Merlin. He bowed to scattered applause as stagehands wheeled a large "disappearing chamber" onstage. A smaller box was pulled to center stage. Merlin spoke.

"That was the final award of the evening. And now, ladies and gentlemen, meet Lovely Little Lola." With a swirl of his cape, Merlin produced a dummy. Lola wore a raggedy blond wig that didn't quite fit. "Care to sing us a tune, my lovely?" Merlin asked the dummy.

The dummy began to sing "Whatever Lola Wants" in a nerve-rattling falsetto.

"That sounds worse than me singing in the shower," George whispered.

Charlie leaned over to Pat and George. "See what I mean? That guy is terrible. His mouth moves more than hers does, and he can't carry a tune in a sedan chair."

Merlin reached for a glass of water. The song stopped abruptly with his first gulp. After a moment, it continued. Pat, George, and Charlie noticed that Lola's voice had changed and become quite lovely. Even Merlin looked surprised. Although Lola's lips had stopped moving, the song seemed to come right from her.

First Pat, then Charlie, then George looked at Edgar. Edgar's lips were moving slightly, in sync with the song. His eyes were bright and there was a smile on his face.

"Look at Edgar. He's coming out of it," Charlie said happily as the song ended.

Onstage, Merlin sensed that something was going wrong. He hurried into his finale. "If one Lovely Little Lola is this good, imagine how good two Lovely Little Lolas could be." He wrestled Lola into the smaller box and slammed the lid. Lola's head and feet hung limply out the

sides. Merlin snickered evilly and produced a huge saw.

Edgar's mouth moved slightly as Lola said, "Oh, no! Please don't saw me in half." Edgar leaped to his feet. Lola's voice cried out, "Please stop!"

Merlin sneered at the dummy as he started to saw. "It won't hurt, my dearest. . . . not for long."

Charlie looked up at Edgar, then back to Lola. "That's not Lola. That's Lolly!" he gasped. "And Merlin's really going to saw her in half. Come on."

Charlie and Edgar led the charge toward the stage as Pat and George brought up the rear. Merlin kept sawing. *We'll never reach the stage in time*, Pat thought.

"Hey Lolly, is that your hair or did you lose a fight with an eggbeater?" Charlie called out, stalling for time.

Merlin stopped sawing and squinted into the glaring lights. Beside him, Lolly's voice answered, "Charles! Is that your nose or are you eating a banana?"

"Lolly, you fugitive from a four-alarm fire, for two cents, I'd . . ."

"For two cents you'd do anything. Get back on the woodpile where you belong."

As Edgar and Charlie reached the stage, there was silence from the audience. You could hear a pin drop.

"Charlie!"

"Edgar!"

"Lolly!"

Charlie and Edgar embraced Lolly, at least the parts of her that stuck out of the box. The audience cheered.

Pat and George spared only a glance for the tender scene before heading for Merlin. Backing away, Merlin shouted over the din, "And now, ladies and gentlemen, I, the Great Merlin, shall disappear . . ."

Merlin rushed into the disappearing chamber, slamming the door shut. There was an enormous bang and a big puff of smoke enveloped the box. Pat and George dove into the murky cloud. When the smoke cleared, the box stood alone on the stage. The audience held its breath. Suddenly, the door was thrown open and George emerged, leading Merlin out in handcuffs. Pat followed, carrying a dummy, also in cuffs. The dummy had been hidden in the box throughout the act, handy for a quick getaway.

"Floyd Snerd, I presume," George said as he unceremoniously tore off the wig that was a part of Snerd's disguise. Pat removed a similar wig from the dummy.

Edgar walked up to them and said, "My old nemesis Snerd, and your dummy, Nosebleed."

"Yeah, it's me," Nosebleed bleated. "What's it to you?"

"And yes, it is I," snarled Snerd. "America's best-kept secret, ventriloquism-wise." He sneered at Pat and George. "You have foiled me. I almost ended Bergman's career. It would have been my greatest triumph."

"But the key word is 'almost,' you cad," Edgar said.

"So you got me." Snerd looked unrepentant. "But you must admit, it would have been a heckuva finish."

"Not as good as the finish we've got planned for you," Pat said. "It's probably the longest run you'll ever have . . . about twenty-five years."

Pat, George, Edgar, Charlie and Lolly did a high five. Then they remembered the audience. For a moment the Mathnetters were embarrassed, until they noticed the entire audience doing high fives, too.

It had turned out to be a lovely evening. Lolly and Edgar were both home at last.

* * *

The next morning, Pat and George were making out their final reports when the door opened and Edgar, Charlie and Lolly came in. There were hugs all around. Edgar announced they were leaving on a big tour through the West and along the Yukon in Alaska.

"We can't thank you enough, Mathnetters," Edgar

said. "I don't know what happened to me, but the doctors have given me a clean bill of health."

"We call it 'Lolly-Loss Syndrome,'" Lolly piped up. "It's being written up in the *New England Journal of Ventriloquism*. I'm thinking of asking for a raise."

Edgar smiled at Pat and George. "She'll be lucky if she gets a better suitcase."

Everyone laughed and said good-bye. As Edgar and his act were leaving, George called out, "Call us when you get back from Alaska, Charlie."

Pat groaned, waiting for it. Sure enough . . .

"Yukon bet we will," Charlie answered.

DUM DE DUM DUM

EPILOGUE

Floyd Snerd and Nosebleed, alias Merlin and the Munchkins, were tried in Manhattan in and for the State of New York. Snerd was found guilty of a 107.15, forgery in the first degree; a 155.40, grand larceny in the second degree; and a 110.00, trying to saw a dummy in half. Nosebleed was found guilty of being a dummy and hanging with a bad ventriloquist. They are both in state prison, where Nosebleed is studying law, hoping to become a mouthpiece.

ACTIVITIES

SEEING STARS

Pat and George gave Charlie
this star to put on his
dressing room door:

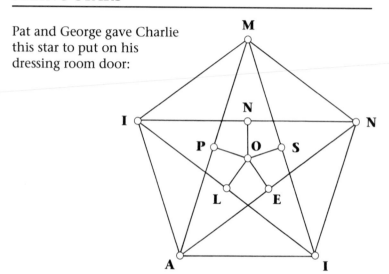

They thought it would remind him of their adventure, because this star is actually a graph with points that form a
Hamiltonian Circuit. Begin at the topmost point and trace a
path that passes through each point only once, before re-
turning to the first point.

Figuring out a Hamiltonian circuit is harder than it looks, so
here's a hint: If you list the points in the order of the correct
path, they'll spell out the name of a city where Edgar was
accused of burgling a bank, plus the first initial of that city's
state.

To celebrate the wrap-up of another Mathnet case, our intrepid detectives visited their favorite ice cream shop for a cone.

Here's the list of flavors:

Deep Dark Vanilla

Chocolate Midnight

Pickle Passion

Citrus Serenade

Triple Fudge Mustard Melody

Mint Chocolate Chip

Ambrosial Anchovy

Banana Bit Explosion

Kreamy Karamel Ketchup

Pineapple Swirl

Liver & Onions Overload

George is a three-scooper (with jimmies). How many cones would he have to try in order to sample every possible combination of three scoops? (Hint: How did the Mathnetters figure out the number of possible suitcase combinations?)

Pat is strictly a two-scooper. How many cones would she have to snarf to try every combination of two flavors?

And Benny outdoes them both—four scoops, minimum.

MONEY MARKET

On their next case the Mathnetters get a tip-off that a gang of counterfeiters is in town. Pat and George go undercover as bogus-bill buyers in order to bust the ring. As you can see, everyone in the gang is offering a different deal. Pat and George have $1,000 to spend and want to get the most for their moola. Which counterfeiter is offering the best bargain?

ANSWERS

1. MINNEAPOLIS M 2. Pat would have to scarf 121 cones to sample every combination (11 flavors, 2 scoops—11 to the second power). George would only have to go back to the shop 1,331 times (11 to the third power). Benny would have to work his way through 14,641 cones. He's still got 17 to go. 3. C— The $1,000 bills were the best bargain. Pat and George could by $10,000 worth. Immediately after making the buy, Pat and George arrested all five gang members for counterfeiting. E was also charged with false advertising.